BATMAN™ TEENAGE MUTANT NINJA TURTLES
ADVENTURES

Raintree is an imprint of Capstone Global Library Limited, a company incorporated in England and Wales having its registered office at 264 Banbury Road, Oxford, OX2 7DY – Registered company number: 6695582

www.raintree.co.uk
myorders@raintree.co.uk

BATMAN/TEENAGE MUTANT NINJA TURTLES ADVENTURES. JULY 2017. FIRST PRINTING. © 2019 Viacom International Inc. and DC Comics. All Rights Reserved. Nickelodeon, TEENAGE MUTANT NINJA TURTLES, and all related titles, logos and characters are trademarks of Viacom International Inc. © 2019 Viacom Overseas Holdings C.V. All Rights Reserved. Nickelodeon, TEENAGE MUTANT NINJA TURTLES, and all related titles, logos and characters are trademarks of Viacom Overseas Holdings C.V. Based on characters created by Peter Laird and Kevin Eastman. DC LOGO, BATMAN and all related characters and elements © & ™ DC Comics. All Rights Reserved. © 2019 Idea and Design Works, LLC. The IDW logo is registered in the U.S. Patent and Trademark Office. IDW Publishing, a division of Idea and Design Works, LLC. Editorial offices: 2765 Truxtun Road, San Diego, CA 92106. Any similarities to persons living or dead are purely coincidental. With the exception of artwork used for review purposes, none of the contents of this publication may be reprinted without the permission of Idea and Design Works, LLC. Printed in Korea. IDW Publishing does not read or accept unsolicited submissions of ideas, stories, or artwork.

Originally published as BATMAN/TEENAGE MUTANT NINJA TURTLES ADVENTURES issue #4.

Special thanks to Jim Chadwick, Joan Hilty, Linda Lee, and Kat van Dam for their invaluable assistance. All rights reserved. No part of this publication may be produced in whole or in part, or stored in a retrieval system, or transmitted in any form or by any means, electronic, mechanical, photocopying, recording, or otherwise, without written permissions of the publisher.

Edited by Chris Harbo and Gena Chester
Designed by Hilary Wacholz
Production by Kathy McColley
Originated by Capstone Global Library Ltd
Printed and bound in India

ISBN 978 1 4747 6650 0
22 21 20 19 18
10 9 8 7 6 5 4 3 2 1

British Library Cataloguing in Publication Data
A full catalogue record for this book is available from the British Library.

Batman created by Bob Kane with Bill Finger

BATMAN TEENAGE MUTANT NINJA TURTLES ADVENTURES

TO LAUGH SO NOT TO CRY

WRITER: MATTHEW K. MANNING | ARTIST: JON SOMMARIVA
INKER: SEAN PARSONS | COLOURIST: LEONARDO ITO

a Capstone company — publishers for children

EW YORK CITY. THE EAST VILLAGE.
OW FLOODED WITH FEAR GAS.
HELP! HELP ME!
I'M SO HUNGRY! WHY WON'T YOU LET ME EAT?!
GET THEM OFF!
MONSTER! YOU'RE A—
I CAN'T BREATHE! THERE'S NO AIR!
HIS EYES! HIS EYES!
OFF! OFF OF ME!
KEEP THE SNAKES AWAY. PLEASE.
WHY ARE THEY LAUGHING?!
CRANE!

CRA—
MONARCH THEATRE
THE MARK
TICKETS
HMPH.
GREAT.
...BRUCE...
...MY BOY...
ALFRED!
WHY... WHY DID YOU GO? WHY ABANDON... GOTHAM?

YOU LEFT US ALONE...
...WITH THEM.
NO, I...
WHACK

ELSEWHERE...
TERRY'S TACOS AND TAXIDERMY.
MR. J?
WHO IS THIS? I'M NOT INTERESTED IN CHANGING MY CABLE PROVIDER.
IT'S ME, YOUR LITTLE HARLEY CAKES!
HARLEY! WHY DIDN'T YOU SAY SO? IT'S BEEN AGES!
TWENTY WHOLE MINUTES!
SO HOW GOES THE NIGHT'S ERRAND, DOLL? THE BOYS AT THE ZOO SAID THEY HAD SOME LUCK, SO HOW'D YOU MAKE OUT?
FANTASTIC! I GOTTA TELL YA', I LOVE THIS PLACE!
NO SUPER PEOPLE IN CAPES. NO DISGRUNTLED SIDEKICKS. NOT EVEN A HARD-AS-NAILS POLICE COMMISSIONER WITH A HEART OF GOLD.
SO YOU FOUND ALL THE NECESSARY... INGREDIENTS?
ENOUGH FOR A BATCH OF JOKER GAS TO KEEP THE WHOLE CITY IN STITCHES!
LITERALLY!
TOXIC
TOXIC
TOXIC
TOXIC
TOXIC
TOXIC

THE JOKER.
FZZT
YEAH. THIS ISN'T GOOD.
REALLY? I KINDA LIKE THE NEW LOOK.
FZZT
I MEAN SURE, THEY WANT TO KILL AND/OR MAIM US, BUT THEY'RE ALL SUPER FRIENDLY ABOUT IT.
IT'S LIKE REALLY GOOD CUSTOMER SERVICE.
GUYS, I THINK FOUND METHING.
IS IT A CREEPY GRINNING FOOTBOT?
BECAUSE I THINK WE'VE ALL FOUND THOSE GUYS, DONNIE.
NO, SERIOUSLY, I NEED A MINUTE WITH THIS.
IT'S... I DON'T KNOW WHAT IT IS.
BUT THIS DOESN'T LOOK LIKE KRAANG TECH.
FZZT
TAKE TWO.
KIAI!
WE'VE GOT THIS.

SO THIS JOKER GUY, HE'S ANOTHER ONE OF THE ESCAPED CONVICTS BATMAN WAS TELLING US ABOUT?
WORST OF THE WORST.
AND NOW HE'S RUNNING THE FOOT CLAN.
IF THAT'S WHO THESE GUYS ARE, I THINK IT'S A SAFE BET.
WAIT, LET THAT ONE GET AWAY. THAT WAY WE CAN FOLLOW IT TO—
FZZZT
FZZZT

HEY!
DUDE. THIS IS THE SHREDDER. WE'VE KNOWN WHERE HIS HIDEOUT IS FOR LIKE, YEARS.

THIS IS THE WEIRDEST DIMENSION EVER.
IT'S... COMPLICATED.

JOKER. THIS SHREDDER GUY.
YEAH.
WE CAN'T DO THIS ALONE.

"I'LL MAKE THE CALL."
...UNHH...
...WHERE?
OH, YOU DON'T WANT TO KNOW THE ANSWER TO THAT ONE, I'M AFRAID.
...UNHH...
KEEP IT AWAY. I MEAN IT.
I'M SORRY.
GET THE BUGS AWAY. GET THE BUGS AWAY.
I'M SO, SO SORRY.
I BELIEVE THIS IS WORST NIGHTMARE TERRAIN.
AND THE GANG'S ALL HERE.

NO.
BEEP BEEP
BATMAN, CAN YOU HEAR ME?
WE NEED YOUR HELP.
I CAN'T... GOTHAM... I...
THIS IS A BIG ONE.
IT'S THE JOKER.
WHAT'S THE MATTER, DARK KNIGHT DETECTIVE? NO FINAL WORDS?
YOU'RE...
YES? DO SPEAK UP.
YOU'RE NO JOKER.
WHACK

HRRR—
-RAHHH!
SHINK
STOP THAT! STOP WHAT YOU'RE DOING!
GET BACK! KEEP BACK OR I'LL... I'LL...
AHH!
FWASH
PANT PANT

TOXIC
WHUNK
C'MON, SMALL WONDER! WATCH WHATCHA' DOING, ALREADY!
THOSE ARE HIGHLY VOLATILE CHEMICALS YOU'RE MANHANDLING.
OR IS IT ROBOT-HANDLING?
ROBOTMAN-HANDLING?
HEY! DON'T YOU WALK AWAY WHEN I'M TALKING AT YOU!
TOXIC CHEM
WHY, I HAVE A GOOD MIND TO—
YOUR MIND IS A LOT OF THINGS, HARLEY. BUT GOOD ISN'T ONE OF THEM.

BATGIRL! AM I GLAD TO SEE YOU, RED!
THINGS HAVE GOTTEN OUT OF HAND, EVEN FOR ME. YOU DON'T KNOW WHAT HE'S PLANNING.

HERE, SEE FOR YOURSELF.
WHAT HE'S DOING, IT'S JUST...
...JUST...

...MONSTROUS!
BUD.
LOU.
What happens when you leave the Joker alone with a giant tub of mutagen.

—GET IT? WE PUT THE GAS IN PEANUT BRITTLE JARS, AND SEND 'EM TO OLD FOLKS' HOMES ALL OVER THE CITY.
AND WHEN UNSUSPECTING EUNICE OPENS UP HER SWEET TREAT...

...EVERYBODY *SMILES!*
WHY NOT JUZZZT POLLUTE THE WATER ZZZUPPLY OR—
WHY DO I DO ANYTHING, REALLY?
HEH HEH HEH

CRASH
UH OH. IS IT THAT SAME BAT-TIME ALREADY?

THAT'S STRANGE.
I DON'T REMEMBER ORDERING SHELLFISH.

WHUMP
HEE HEE
WE SHOULD GET OUT THERE AND BUST SOME–
NO.
THAT CLOWN MAKES MOCKERY OF FOOT.
THIS FIGHT BELONG TO HIM.
ALONE.

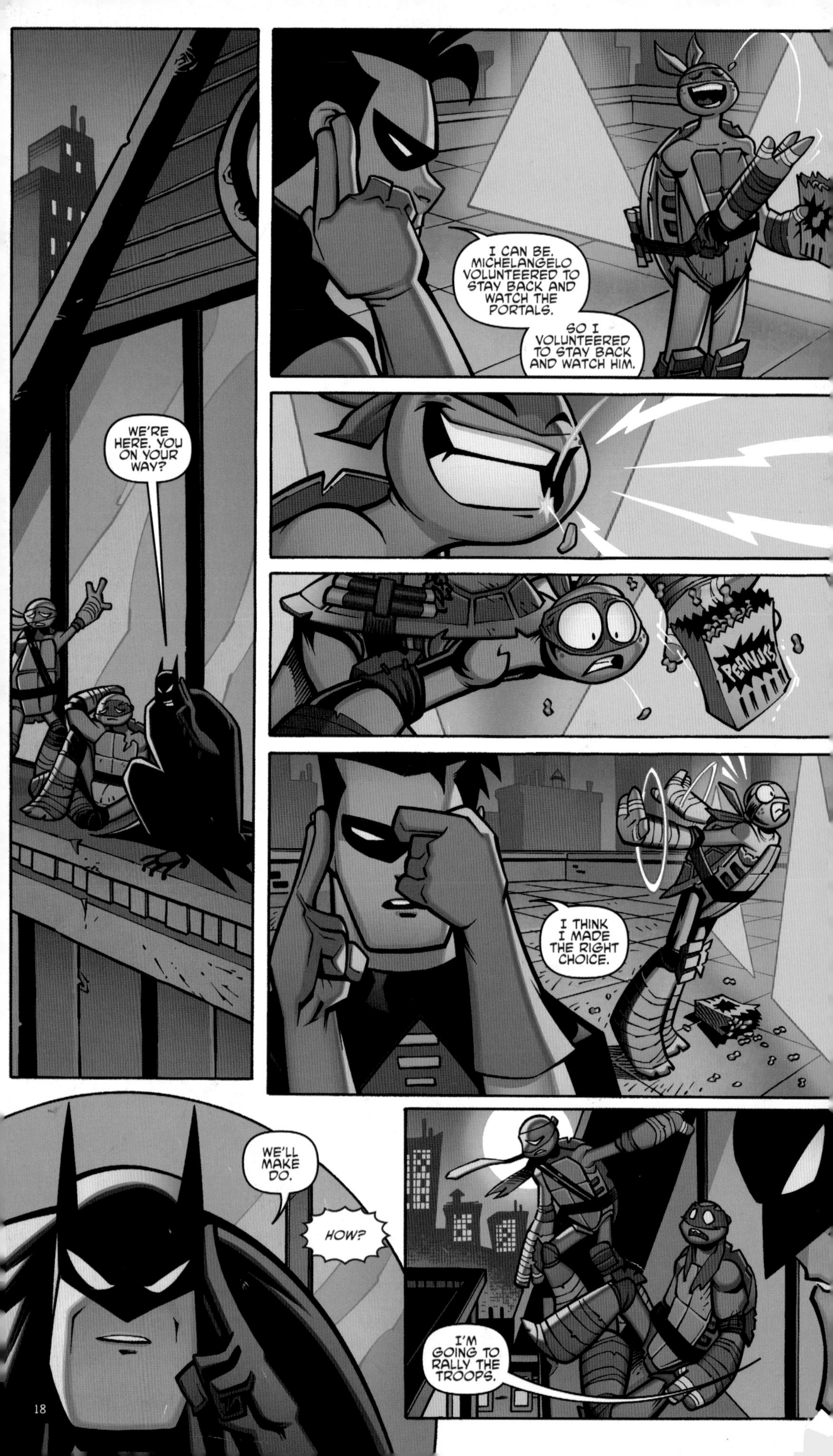
WE'RE HERE. YOU ON YOUR WAY?
I CAN BE. MICHELANGELO VOLUNTEERED TO STAY BACK AND WATCH THE PORTALS.
SO I VOLUNTEERED TO STAY BACK AND WATCH HIM.
PEANUTS
I THINK I MADE THE RIGHT CHOICE.
WE'LL MAKE DO.
HOW?
I'M GOING TO RALLY THE TROOPS.

I'M HEADED DOWN THERE. AND I NEED YOUR HELP.
IT'S ALREADY TOO LATE.
WHATEVER YOU'RE EXPERIENCING, WHATEVER YOU'RE SEEING, IT ISN'T REAL.
I'VE DEALT WITH SCARECROW'S FEAR GAS BEFORE. TOO MANY TIMES.
IT'S ALL JUST CHEMICALS REACTING WITH YOUR BRAIN.
"BUT THAT MAN DOWN THERE? THAT CLOWN? HE IS VERY, VERY REAL.
"AND HE IS WORSE THAN ANYTHING IN YOUR HEAD."
YOU HAVE TWO OPTIONS. SEE THE WORLD HOW SCARECROW WANTS YOU TO...
...OR STOP IT FROM BECOMING THAT WAY.
I'VE MADE MY CHOICE.

CRASH
HA!
TWHACK
WHUMP
UM... THANKS.
YOU WOULD HAVE DONE THE SAME FOR ME.
HEE HEE HEE

HEE HEE
I CAN'T DO THIS, MAN. I CAN'T DO THIS.
YOU HEARD HIM, RAPH. NONE OF WHAT WE'RE SEEING IS REAL.
WE'RE NINJA. TRAINED BY THE BEST OF THE BEST.
THINK OF MASTER SPLINTER. THINK OF WHAT HE TAUGHT US.
HE COULD SEE THROUGH THIS IN A SECOND.
...UHNNN...
...SPLINTER.
AND IF HE COULD, THEN SO CAN WE.
HEE

RED LIGHT!
HEY, MA, LOOK AT ME!
NOW I DIDN'T KNOW YOU WERE COMING, BATSY, SO I ONLY HAVE A TINY BIT OF THE OLD JOKER GAS TO SHARE.
IT'S NOT MUCH, JUST ENOUGH TO FILL THE ROOM AND MAKE A MOCKERY OF—
CLANG
MY IT'S LATE. THINK I'LL COUNT SOME SHEEP.
WHUMP
IT'S OVER.
GO.
TAKE YOUR CLOWNS AND GET OUT.
OUR FIGHT IS FOR ANOTHER DAY.

I MEAN, IS THAT EVEN POSSIBLE?
SHRUGGING OFF THE JOKER'S GAS LIKE THAT?
THE HONEST ANSWER: NO. NOT AT ALL.
I DON'T KNOW WHAT YOUR BUDDY SHREDDER IS MADE OF, BUT HE MUST HAVE A WILL LIKE AN IRON—
IT'S NOT THE KRAANG!
WHAT?
THIS WHOLE TIME, WE'VE JUST ASSUMED THAT THE KRAANG ARE BEHIND THESE PORTALS. BUT IT'S NOT THEM.
I'VE BEEN STUDYING THIS BEACON, AND I'M SURE OF IT NOW.
IT'S SOMEBODY ELSE. SOMEONE WHO TAPPED INTO THE KRAANG'S FREQUENCY.
THESE BEACONS ARE RECEPTORS. *MANMADE* RECEPTORS.
THEY'RE BUILT TO CONTROL MINDS FROM... FROM SOMEWHERE FAR AWAY.
AND I'D BE WILLING TO BET THAT THE METALS ARE FROM YOUR DIMENSION, BATMAN.
DOES THAT SOUND FAMILIAR? I MEAN...

"...DO YOU KNOW ANYONE WHO COULD PULL THAT OFF?"
"WHY, SOMETIMES I'VE BELIEVED AS MANY AS SIX IMPOSSIBLE THINGS BEFORE BREAKFAST."
10/6
THE MAD HATTER.
The final Arkham Asylum Escapee. Inventor. Genius.
The maddest of them all.

CREATORS

MATTHEW K. MANNING

THE AUTHOR OF THE AMAZON BEST-SELLING *BATMAN: A VISUAL HISTORY*, MATTHEW K. MANNING HAS CONTRIBUTED TO MANY COMIC BOOKS, INCLUDING *BEWARE THE BATMAN, SPIDER-MAN UNLIMITED, PIRATES OF THE CARIBBEAN: SIX SEA SHANTIES, JUSTICE LEAGUE ADVENTURES, LOONEY TUNES* AND *SCOOBY-DOO, WHERE ARE YOU?* WHEN NOT WRITING COMICS, MANNING OFTEN WRITES BOOKS ABOUT COMICS, AS WELL AS A SERIES OF YOUNG READER BOOKS STARRING SUPERMAN, BATMAN AND THE FLASH. HE CURRENTLY LIVES IN NORTH CAROLINA, USA, WITH HIS WIFE, DOROTHY, AND THEIR TWO DAUGHTERS, LILLIAN AND GWENDOLYN.
VISIT HIM ONLINE AT WWW.MATTHEWKMANNING.COM.

JON SOMMARIVA

JON SOMMARIVA WAS BORN IN SYDNEY, AUSTRALIA. HE HAS BEEN DRAWING COMIC BOOKS SINCE 2002. HIS WORK CAN BE SEEN IN *GEMINI, REXODUS, TMNT ADVENTURES* AND *STAR WARS ADVENTURES,* AMONG OTHER COMICS. WHEN HE IS NOT DRAWING, HE ENJOYS WATCHING FILMS AND PLAYING WITH HIS SON, FELIX.

GLOSSARY

abandon leave and never return

beacon small radio or signal transmitter, or traditionally a fire or light for a message or warning

chemical substance used in or produced by chemistry

commissioner official who leads a us government department such as the police force

convict someone in prison for committing a crime

customer person who buys goods or services

dimension another world or reality that we are unable to detect or measure

disgruntled displeased or annoyed

errand task or job to deliver or pick up something

frequency speed of vibrations of an electromagnetic wave used for radio communication

ingredient item used to make something, such as food for a recipe

maim injure someone so that their body is damaged for life

mockery misrepresentation of something meant to be funny or insulting

rally organize or prepare fighters for action

receptor something that receives signals or information

terrain ground

volatile unstable

DISCUSSION QUESTIONS AND WRITING PROMPTS

1. WHY DO YOU THINK BATMAN TAKES OFF HIS GAS MASK?

2. WRITE A SCENE THAT DETAILS WHAT THE JOKER PLANS TO DO WITH THE LAUGHING GAS.

3. THE JOKER MADE MUTANTS WITH MUTAGEN. IF YOU COULD MAKE YOUR OWN MUTANTS, WHAT WOULD THEY LOOK LIKE? WHAT WOULD YOU USE THEM FOR?

4. DONATELLO HAS JUST ANNOUNCED THAT THE KRAANG ARE NOT BEHIND THESE PORTALS. WHAT DO YOU THINK IS GOING ON IN THE MINDS OF EACH OF THE CHARACTERS BELOW? HOW DO THEY FEEL ABOUT THIS NEW INFORMATION?

BATMAN TEENAGE MUTANT NINJA TURTLES ADVENTURES

READ THEM ALL!

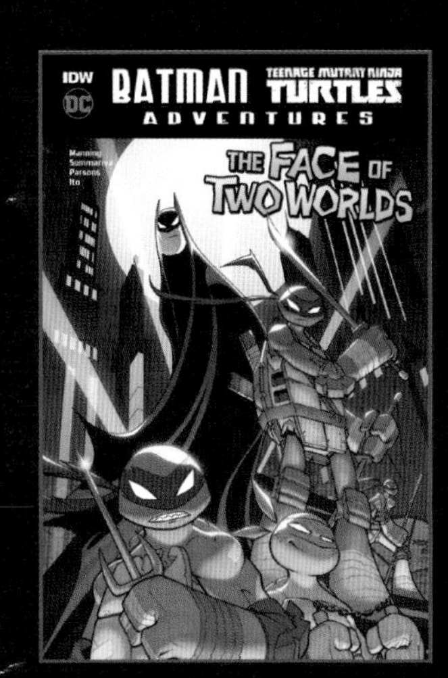

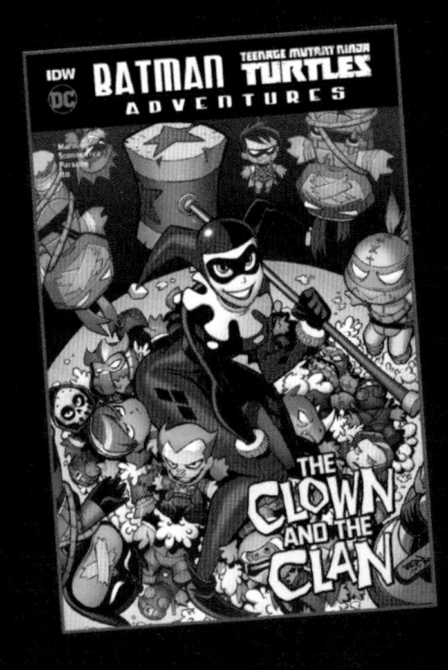

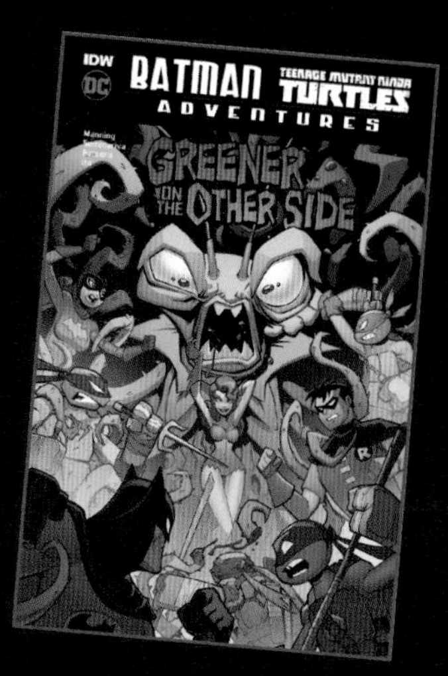

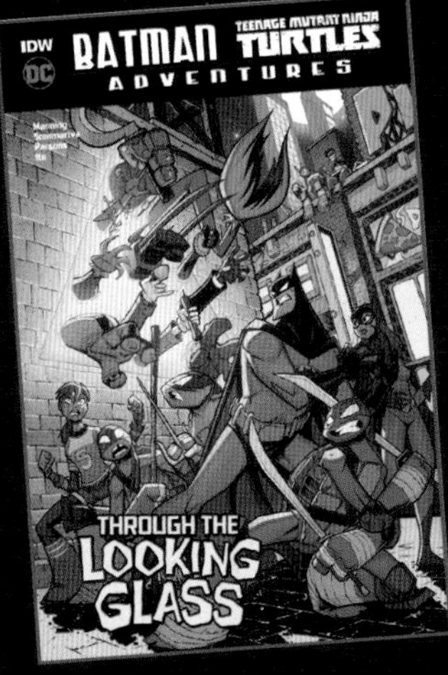

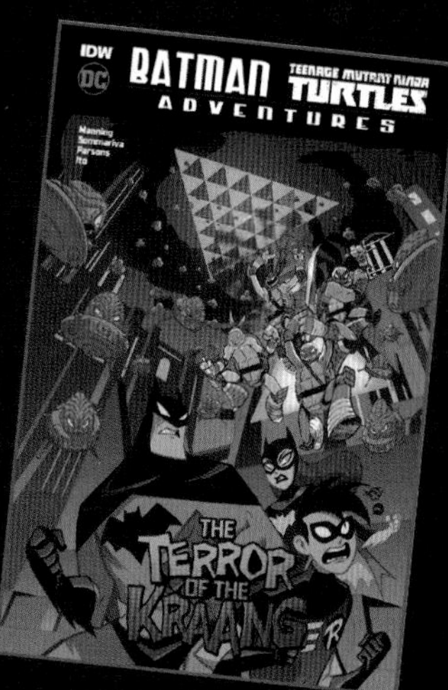

ONLY FROM

raintree

a Capstone company — publishers for children

BATMAN™ TEENAGE MUTANT NINJA TURTLES™
ADVENTURES